# Believe in the MAGIC of BLACKBURN Town Centre

Children's Literature FESTIVALS

It is Saturday, and Heidi has promised to take Peggy and Imtiaz to Blackburn Museum. Peggy has been longing to see the wonderful collection of coins that were donated to the museum by local rope maker Edward Hart. It is a huge collection, which includes coins from the reigns of different Roman emperors, and Peggy is fascinated by it. Imtiaz wants to know more about the Hart family and the history.

Heidi sits down to read her book, giving Peggy and Imtiaz time to look around and explore.
"Let's begin in the Egyptian room," suggests Imtiaz. "They have a real Egyptian mummy."
"Wow, ok!" agrees Peggy.

They venture into the room and see the mummy inside a glass case.
"Look!" exclaims Imtiaz, pointing to a mural on the wall. He walks up to it.
"This almost looks as though we could walk into it."
He touches the mural and his hand disappears through it, so he decides to step his foot through it too.

"Wow, Peggy have you seen this? Let's go down here, it looks like a secret passage."
As she enters the passage, Peggy sees a shiny gold coin on the floor.
"Oooo!" she says. "That gold coin is rolling away." They both follow the coin and before they realise, they have walked so far down the passage, it takes them outside.

"It's very noisy out here," cries Imtiaz. "The floor is all cobbled. Where are we?  Wait a minute. That building looks like the Town Hall and that one looks like the cinema, but all the people are wearing different clothes.  How fun!"
"We must go back inside or Heidi will be cross with us; we were supposed to stay in the museum," pleads Peggy.
"Yes, but it feels like we still are, in a way," says Imtiaz.

"Look! There's the gold coin rolling over in that direction, towards the town centre. Oh no that bird has just swooped down and taken it. We must tell someone quickly. There's a policeman over there. Perhaps he can help," suggests Peggy.
"Don't be so ridiculous, he's not going to be interested; he might think we are silly.  We will never catch a bird. Anyway, where are we? Look at the date on that clock, Peggy. I think that we have gone back in time," declares Imtiaz.
"Never! That's not possible," replies Peggy. "Well I'm going to try to talk to the policeman, as the coin must be from the museum."

Peggy makes her way towards the policeman. "Excuse me, please can you help us?" she asks.
"What seems to be the problem?" enquires the policeman.
"We have lost a gold coin, and we saw a large bird swoop down and take it. It flew off in that direction," Peggy tells him.
"Oh no, not again," sighs the policeman. "This is a well-known, trained bird that belongs to a trickster in the town. I know exactly where he will have taken it."

"Where?" demands Peggy excitedly.
"The Fire Station Tower," answers the policeman.
"I can't see a tower. We will never get the coin back," says Peggy despondently.
"You are unable to see it, as it is in the future. They started building it in 1915," declares the policeman.
Imtiaz looks around puzzled, "I don't understand."
"Come down to the Police Station with me and I will make some inquiries," offers the policeman. "My name is PC Peel, by the way."

Peggy and Imtiaz follow him to the Police Station.
"Who are you here with?" asks PC Peel.
"We are with our foster mum, Heidi. She is reading her book in the museum," explains Peggy.
PC Peel regards Imtiaz. "What's that hanging out of your pocket young man?"
Imtiaz looks a bit sheepish. "It's a piece of rope that I found on the floor in the museum."

"Hmmmm," mutters PC Peel. "So, you both say that you were in the museum. You didn't by any chance manage to stray into a long passageway, did you?"
"Yes, we did. Why?" demands Imtiaz.
"You have travelled back in time to the 1800s," responds PC Peel.
"No way! How can that happen?" wonders Peggy.
"It's the magic of the secret passageway. And when this happens, it is usually to help with something that's happening in the present day. Time will stand still where you have come from, until you have found what you came for," reveals PC Peel.
"Well, we are experiencing a pandemic in our town," answers Peggy.
"Not just our town though. This is all over the world," corrects Imtiaz. "So, do you think that the gold coin may be in the Fire Station Tower?"
"It could be, but that wasn't completed until 1921, so you will have to travel forward in time to take a look," replies PC Peel.
"And how are we going to do that?" retorts Peggy.
"Take a look at the rope you have in your pocket," says PC Peel. They all look down at the rope and can see that it is glowing. "It's the Lambeth Rope, which was invented by the Hart family."
"Oh yes, we read all about it in the museum. Their rope was used all over the world," agrees Peggy.
Imtiaz takes the rope from his pocket.
"Now," says PC Peel. "You both need to hold on to the rope, close your eyes and concentrate on the place where you want to go, in this case the Fire Station Tower."

The children both hold on to the rope, close their eyes and think of the Tower. They feel a slight tingling and, within seconds, they find themselves at the top of the Fire Station Tower, looking out over Blackburn.
They hear a voice. "Hello, who's there?" The children stay quiet. They hear footsteps getting louder, coming up the stone steps, and can see a light shining.
"Hello, I'm Fireman John Davis 52-443. What are you two doing up here?"
"I'm Peggy and this is Imtiaz. We are looking for a big, black bird, who has stolen a shiny gold coin from the museum."
"Oh, not that bird again! I was hoping that it would have been captured by now. I haven't noticed anything around here recently though. Come with me and we can have a look around the engine house," offers Fireman Davis.

They climb down through the trapdoor, down the ladder and stairs of the Tower. They can't see anything in the engine house, but are both excited to see the large, brass fireman's pole.

Fireman Davis lets the children slide down the brass pole. "Well I don't think that there is anything here. Have you tried King George's Hall, Blackburn College around Blakey Moor, or the Library?" he suggests.

"Let's try King George's Hall first. What year was that built?" asks Imtiaz.

"It was finished in 1921 as well, just like this place," replies Fireman Davis.

"We must go there.  Or could the bird have travelled through to a different period in time?" wonders Peggy.

"I think that's for you to find out," smiles Fireman Davis.

"Thank you for your help Fireman Davis," chorus the children.

"That's ok.  Good luck with your mission! Goodbye," he shouts.

They both hold on to the Lambeth rope, close their eyes and think of King George's Hall. They land in the Assembly Hall, which is now the Windsor Suite, where there is a performance of Snow White & the Seven Dwarfs in full flow. They are both mesmerised by the show.
Imtiaz nudges Peggy. "Come on, let's not forget why we are here. We need to have a look around, but where do we start? Look out, there is an usher over there. We'll be in trouble if we are seen," he whispers.
They both tiptoe over to near the stage and sneak into the dressing room area.

Peggy walks past a mirror. "Oh, I think this is the mirror that they are using on stage and maybe it should be out there already."
The mirror replies, "I'm the back up, just in case the other mirror breaks."
"Oh wow! The mirror can speak," exclaims Peggy.

The mirror looks indignant. "Of course I can! I am a magic mirror. What are you two doing here anyway?"
"We are looking for a gold coin that was stolen by a large, black bird. I don't suppose you have seen anything?" asks Peggy.
"Well, now that you mention it, yes, that bird is always up to no good. But I haven't seen any coins. The bird is always hanging around and stealing things," explains the mirror.
"Do you know where it went?" Imtiaz questions the mirror.
It replies, "I really don't know, but it's always travelling through different periods in time to avoid being caught."
"Ok, thank you anyway. Come on Imtiaz, we need to try Blakey Moor School. My grandmother used to go to the school and swim in the pool there," says Peggy.

The two children walk out of the door and head into Blakey Moor School, which is next door to King George's Hall. "Wow," cries Imtiaz. "I didn't know that there was a swimming pool here."
"Yes. I told you my grandmother used to swim here," exclaims Peggy.

They both see a silhouette of the bird on the wall. "There it is, look!" shouts Imtiaz.
The bird moves quickly and disappears in a cloud of steam. "Oh no! Where has it gone now?" moans Imtiaz. "Let's try the College. We can walk there."
"Yes," agrees Peggy. "But won't it be quicker if we hold on to the rope? Let's go to the top floor."

They both hold on to the magic Lambeth rope. They arrive on the top floor of the College.
"It's very quiet up here. How are we ever going to find the bird or the coin? This is hopeless," sighs Imtiaz. "We must get back to the museum. Heidi will wonder where we are. We are in the middle of a pandemic too, Peggy, have you forgotten?"
"No, I haven't. Things are improving, Imtiaz or we wouldn't be allowed into the museum in the first place," argues Peggy. "We mustn't give up. Heidi always says that to us. And anyway, remember what PC Peel said. He said that time would stand still in 2020 until we return back to the museum."

Both Peggy and Imtiaz sit down and decide to map out places to check. "Ok, we should try the Cathedral, as I'm sure that the bird will go as high as possible to try and stay out of our way. If we have no luck there, we can try the Market, the Library and The Mall," offers Peggy.
"Why don't we try The Mall first? We may be able to get some help. What year shall we go to? Shall we hold on to the rope and see where it takes us?" suggests Imtiaz.
"Ok," Peggy replies.

They hold on to the Lambeth rope, close their eyes and, seconds later, find themselves in the shopping centre, with very brightly coloured mannequins in all the shop windows. "What year do you think we are in now?" asks Imtiaz.
"I'm not sure, but looking at the clothes and thinking about mum's photos, it looks like the 1970s," answers Peggy.
It is dark and all the shops are closed. "This is no use. What are we supposed to do?" grumbles Imtiaz.
"Well, maybe the rope transported us here for a reason. Look at the mannequin there, did you see it move?" whispers Peggy.
"Don't be silly," retorts Imtiaz.
"Look, she just waved for us to go over to her," murmurs Peggy.

They both walk over reluctantly. The mannequin suddenly steps through the window. Peggy and Imtiaz gasp.
"Hello children, I do believe that you need help," smiles the mannequin. "I received a message through time."
"Yes, we are in a pandemic in 2020, and we want to just go back, but first we need to find the gold coin, as the policeman told us that it will help bring magic back into our town," explains Peggy in a rush.

"Ok, keep calm. I would suggest we try the Cathedral spire. The bird always likes to go as high as possible to try and deter anyone from following. It's lovely to meet you both by the way. My name is Rowena, and I know that you are Peggy and Imtiaz," says the mannequin.
"Rowena, that's a pretty name," replies Peggy.
"Thank you."
Rowena takes their hands. They all hold on to the magic Lambeth rope and in a flash...

They find themselves at the top of the Cathedral spire. It is 1926.
"Wow! It's spectacular up here," breathes Imtiaz, "but there's no sign of the bird."
"Hold on to the rope, we will try the Market," declares Rowena.

Once again, they hold on to the rope and when they open their eyes, they realise that they are on top of the old clock tower at the Market, with its time ball. The ball was raised to the top of the mast every day and on the stroke of 1.00pm dropped down.
"Oh, we have come too far back in time. We are in 1883. Hold on to the rope," requests Rowena.

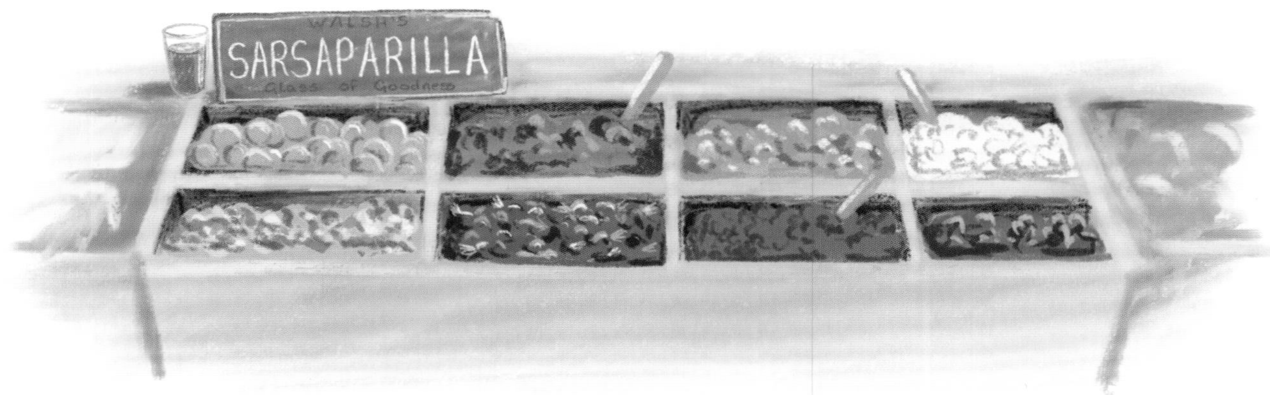


The rope takes them into the main covered market area of the 1960s and The Mall.
"Look at all those sweets," says Peggy, her eyes lighting up.
"And look, there are some gold coins," cries Imtiaz.
"Yes, but they are sweets and not the real thing," corrects Peggy.
"Look at that beautiful dress in the shop window," murmurs Rowena dreamily.
"The bird is over there," says Peggy, pointing. "And it's got something in its mouth."
The bird flies off once again, in the direction of the Library. They all hold on to the rope and close their eyes. "To the library," shouts Peggy.

They arrive in the reference library, with walls and walls of books. "This is amazing, look at all these books," says Imtiaz. "I love reading, can we stay for a while?"
"I really think that we should concentrate on our mission and maybe come back another time. When you return to 2020, the Mayor will be cutting the ribbon to present a new book to the town in two hours' time. It's called *Believe in the Magic of Blackburn Town Centre,"* replies Rowena.
"Look!" exclaims Imtiaz. "The bird is over there at the top of the Town Hall. It has the coin! Quick, hold on to the rope."

They hold on and, in seconds, they are at the top of the Town Hall, and this time the bird doesn't fly away.

The bird looks at them. "Well done, you have completed your mission."
"What?" cries Peggy.
"You were brought out of the museum to help take something positive back into the future with the help of the past. The gold coin belongs back in the Hart collection in the museum. Edward Hart wanted to help to write a story that could bring some magic back into the town centre and for you to be part of the story," explains the bird. "Here is the coin. Hold on to the rope and you will be back in the museum in the Hart Gallery. Heidi, your foster mum, will never know that you were missing, as time has stood still."

"Thank you," they both chorus. They turn and hug Rowena goodbye. They hold on to the Lambeth rope for one final time and close their eyes. Within seconds they are back in the museum in the Hart gallery; the coin and rope are back in the display case.
They hear Heidi's voice. "Peggy, Imtiaz, we are going to be late for the Mayor's presentation. He will be cutting the ribbon for the new book that they are all talking about," she calls.
"Wow, it's all true Imtiaz," whispers Peggy.
"Coming," shouts Imtiaz, grinning at her.

"Have you both enjoyed your visit?" asks Heidi.
"Yes, it's the most amazing place. Please can we come again sometime?" says Peggy.
"Of course," nods Heidi.
Peggy and Imtiaz look at one another with huge beaming smiles.

They all head over to the Town Hall, where the Mayor is standing on a small stage, with a pile of books surrounded by ribbon.

"I now declare *Believe in the Magic of Blackburn Town Centre* book sales open," he booms, and cuts the ribbon. There is a huge cheer from the crowd.